THE TINKLERS THREE

The Perfect Pet
published in 2014 by
Hardie Grant Egmont
Ground Floor, Building 1, 658 Church Street
Richmond, Victoria 3121, Australia
www.hardiegrantegmont.com.au

A CiP record for this title is available from the National Library of Australia.

Text copyright © 2014 MC Badger
Illustration copyright © 2014 Jon Davis
Series design copyright © 2014 Hardie Grant Egmont

Design by Elissa Webb
Illustrations by Jon Davis
based on original characters by Leigh Brown

Printed in Australia by Griffin Press, an Accredited ISO AS/NZS
14001:2004 Environmental Management System printer.

1 3 5 7 9 10 8 6 4 2

The paper this book is printed on is certified against the
Forest Stewardship Council® Standards. Griffin Press holds
FSC chain of custody certification SGS-COC-005088. FSC
promotes environmentally responsible, socially beneficial
and economically viable management of the world's forests.

the TINKLERS THREE

the perfect PET

M·C·BADGER

illustrated by
jon davis

hardie grant EGMONT

CHAPTER ONE

MARCUS TINKLER was used to his sisters doing strange things. After all, one of his sisters thought she was a turtle. (That was his younger sister, Turtle.) The other one thought if you planted a salami in the ground it would grow into a salami tree. (That was his older sister, Mila.) Sometimes, Marcus felt like he was the only normal one in his family.

But let me tell you something:

MARCUS wasn't that NORMAL either.

None of the Tinklers were.

Their parents worked in a travelling circus, so the Tinkler children lived all by themselves in a flat at thirty-three Rushby Road. That's not very normal, now, is it?

On this particular morning, Marcus's sister Mila was doing something *very* strange. She was leaning out the window of the Tinklers' flat, waving a grabby hand around.

Do you know what a grabby hand is? It's a stick with a grabber on the end. Marcus invented it.

The Tinklers often used the grabby hand to feed seed bread to the pigeons.

But today, there wasn't seed bread in the grabby hand. Today there was a banana.

'What are you doing?' Marcus asked Mila. 'Pigeons don't eat bananas.'

'I know that,' said Mila. 'Today I am trying to catch an African grey parrot.'

'But Mila,' said Marcus, 'there aren't any African grey parrots around here. African grey parrots live in Africa.'

'I know that, too,' said Mila. 'But one might be here on holiday. Our city is a very nice place for birds to visit. There are lots of statues for them to sit on. There are also a lot of washing lines with clean laundry for them to poo on.'

'Why do you want to catch an African grey parrot anyway?' Marcus asked.

'Because it's time we got a pet,' Mila said firmly.

'Really?' said Marcus. His eyes lit up. 'It's finally time?'

Turtle had crawled into the room and was looking excited too. The Tinklers had wanted a pet for *ages*. But they also knew that children didn't get pets easily – there were things they had to do first to show they were ready for one. Luckily, Mila knew exactly what these things were.

Mila said that for a whole month before getting a pet there were three rules you had to follow:

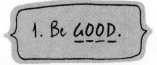

1. Be GOOD.

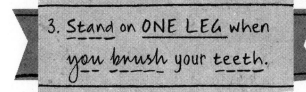

2. Eat an EXTRA bowl of ice-cream EVERY DAY.

3. Stand on ONE LEG when you brush your teeth.

The last one was the most important rule of all.

If they fell over, they'd have to wait even longer before they could get a pet.

Being good for a month was easy.

Marcus did a _GOOD_ job of breaking a vase by playing football inside.

Mila did a _GOOD_ job of using up the milk by spilling it on the kitchen bench.

Turtle did a GREAT job of making the boring grey TV look much prettier by painting it all over with nailpolish.

Eating an extra bowl of ice-cream every day was a bit harder. The Tinklers already ate *a lot* of ice-cream. Sometimes they really didn't feel they could fit in one more bowl. But if it meant they could get a pet, they knew it was worth it.

Standing on one leg while they brushed their teeth was also pretty hard. But then Mila worked out that if you H‍O‍P while standing on one leg it's much easier than standing still.

'It's easier to clean your teeth while hopping too,' she pointed out. 'You just hold the brush still and rub your teeth up against it as you jump.'

Marcus had lost track of how long they had been doing these things. It felt like a very long time.

Marcus had started to wonder if they would ever get a pet, so he was very pleased Mila said they were ready. But there was one thing he wasn't sure about.

'Do we have to get a parrot as a pet?' he asked. 'I want to get a dog. Dogs are friendly and loyal and fun to play with.'

'Grey parrots make very good pets,' said Mila. 'They are super smart. You can teach them to do all kinds of things. If we had one, it could answer the phone for us.'

'Well, I want a **CAMEL** as a pet,' said Turtle. 'Camels have three eyelids, one on top of the other. Animals with three eyelids make the best pets of all. And the best bit is that if we had a camel we could ride on it.'

'I thought you were a turtle,' said Marcus. 'Turtles don't have pets.'

Turtle took a bite out of the lettuce leaf she was holding. 'You are wrong, Marcus,' she said. 'Of course turtles have pets. You just never see them because we keep them inside our shells.'

'How will you keep a camel in your shell?' Marcus asked.

Maybe now you can see why Marcus thought he was the only normal one in his family.

'I have an idea,' said Marcus. 'Let's go to the pet shop. There's one just down the road. That will be a lot easier than trying to catch a pet out the window.'

'But it costs money to buy a pet,' said Mila.

The Tinklers had a lot of their pocket money saved up. But Mila HATED spending it.

'We don't have to buy a pet this time,' said Marcus. 'We can just look and get some ideas.'

Mila thought about this. 'OK,' she said after a minute. 'That sounds like a good idea. And I will bring this with me too.' She pulled the grabby hand back in through the window. It was still holding onto the banana. 'Maybe we will find an African grey parrot on the way there.'

CHAPTER TWO

BECAUSE THE TINKLERS lived on the thirty-third floor, they usually caught the lift when they were going out. Some days they liked to slide down the banister. But sometimes they went down a new way. Today was one of those days.

'Let's try out my new spring slide!' said Marcus.

This was Marcus's latest invention. When it was on the ground it looked like a huge, flat doughnut. But when you held onto one end and put the other end out the window, it turned into a slide. A very *LONG*, very twisty slide.

Now, most parents would tell their children that it was dangerous to go down a very long, very twisty slide. Especially if the slide was thirty-three storeys high. But, of course, the Tinklers' parents were not around.

'I'll go first,' said Marcus, 'because I invented the slide.'

'No, you can't,' said Mila. 'It's a rule.'

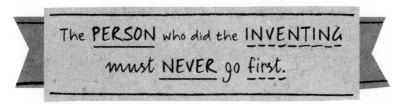

The **PERSON** who did the **INVENTING** must **NEVER** go first.

Mila liked rules. She especially liked making them up.

Marcus didn't argue. He had only just finished putting the slide together that morning. Maybe the glue wasn't dry. If Mila wanted to test it out, he didn't mind!

Mila climbed out the window and onto the slide.

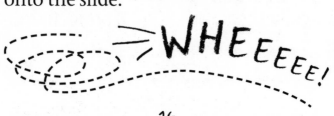

WHEEEEE!

Around and around she went, holding the grabby hand out to one side. It took a very long time for her to pop out at the bottom.

Marcus leant out the window and looked down at Mila.

'How was it?' he called down to her.

'Great!' Mila called back. 'But I'm very dizzy now.'

Marcus already knew that. He could tell from the way Mila was walking. She kept BUMPING into things.

Turtle went next. She took off her cardboard-box shell and climbed into it.

'Turtles always slide this way,' she told Marcus. 'It's faster.'

WHEE!

Turtle went even faster than Mila. Have you ever seen a dizzy turtle? It is very funny.

Marcus went last, and soon he was down on Rushby Road with his sisters.

★ ★ ★

The pet shop was only two blocks away, but Marcus knew it might take a long time to get there.

Sometimes it took the Tinklers a long time to go places because Turtle wanted to crawl.

Sometimes it took a long time because Mila said that it was 'stop and chat with everyone we know' day. That took forever because the Tinklers knew a lot of people.

Sometimes the problem was that the Tinklers were spotted by a Worried Adult.

Now, the Tinklers were very good at looking after themselves. But when some people saw the Tinklers walking along without an adult, they got worried. They started asking questions like: Are you **LOST?**

Or: **WHERE** are your **PARENTS?**

But even when the Tinklers told them that they *weren't* lost and that their parents worked in a circus, the adults never believed them. They always wanted to call the police. It was very annoying!

Luckily, the Tinklers had worked out a good way of dealing with this.

Marcus reminded his sisters about it now, because there was an older woman looking at them and Marcus was pretty sure she was a Worried Adult.

'Look for someone who might be a mum,' said Marcus.

All three Tinklers looked around.

'How about her?' Mila spotted a lady walking along. She looked like she could be a nice mother. Perfect!

The Tinklers Three sneaked up behind her. They didn't get so close that the lady noticed them, but they made sure they were close enough to her that the Worried Adult might *think* she was their mum.

It worked! The Worried Adult walked away.

Once the Tinklers were around the corner, they relaxed and started talking about what kind of pet they wanted.

'It has to be something friendly,' said Marcus. 'It should come when it's called and it should sleep on the end of our beds.'

'It needs to be big enough to ride on,' said Turtle. 'And it should be able to close its nostrils between breaths.'

'No animal can do that!' said Marcus.

'A camel can,' said Turtle.

'Those are all good things,' said Mila. 'But you've forgotten the most important thing.'

'What's that?' asked Marcus.

'It must be a pet that can teach us tricks.'

'You mean a pet that we can teach tricks to,' corrected Marcus.

Mila shook her head. 'No, I don't mean that at all. I want it to teach *us* stuff.

23

If it's a bird I want it to teach us how to fly. If it's a fish I want it to show us how to stay underwater all day.'

'Hmm,' said Marcus. 'I think it will be very hard to find a pet like that.'

Suddenly Turtle stopped walking.

'Why have you stopped?' asked Marcus.

'Because we are here,' said Turtle.

Marcus looked around and saw that Turtle was right. They were standing outside a shop. Written on the window was a sign:

★ WHATEVER PET YOU WANT, ★ WE HAVE IT. ★

Mila smiled. 'Do you see that, Marcus?' she said, pointing at the sign. 'It was a good idea to come here. We'll definitely find the perfect pet in here.'

CHAPTER THREE

THE SHOPKEEPER came over to the Tinklers as they walked in.

'Hello!' he said. 'Can I help you?'

'Yes,' said Mila. 'We are looking for the perfect pet.'

'Well, this is the perfect place to find the perfect pet!' said the shopkeeper. 'Let me show you around.'

The shopkeeper showed the Tinklers a lot of different animals. He showed them some puppies that were rolling around and trying to bite their tails. He showed them some soft little kittens, curled up together in a basket. He showed them some black and white mice, running around in a wheel so fast that their legs were a **blur**.

Marcus thought all these pets were great. But Mila didn't.

'These pets are OK for other people,' she said to the shopkeeper. 'But we are the Tinklers and we need something different. We don't just want an *ordinary* pet. Do you have any crocodiles? Or penguins? Even a silverback gorilla would be fine.'

28

'Something with three eyelids would be best,' added Turtle.

The shopkeeper shook his head. 'I'm sorry,' he said. 'I don't have any animals like that. But I *do* have one more pet here that I'm sure you will love.'

He turned and called out to a teenage girl who was standing behind the shop counter. 'Lucy, where is Miss Waffles?'

'She's here, Dad,' the girl said. She bent down and picked up something from the ground. It was the biggest, FLUFFIEST rabbit Marcus had ever seen.

Marcus looked at Mila as the girl walked over with Miss Waffles in her arms. Mila looked thrilled.

'Oh!' Mila said. 'She's just what I want! Look at her great big eyes and her adorable twitching nose!'

The shopkeeper smiled. 'I knew you'd love Miss Waffles.'

But Mila shook her head. 'I don't mean that boring old rabbit,' she said. 'I mean HER!' Mila flung her arms around the girl holding the rabbit.

'She's not a pet!' said the shopkeeper. 'She's my daughter, Lucy.'

'But she's *perfect* for us!' said Mila. 'She can talk really well. And she came when you called her. She is just what we're looking for.'

'Can she close her nostrils between breaths?' asked Turtle.

'I don't think so,' said Mila, looking at the girl's nose.

'Well then, she's not that perfect,' said Turtle, grumpily.

Marcus agreed with Turtle. 'I'm sure she doesn't want to be our pet, anyway.'

Mila looked at Lucy. 'You would LOVE to be our pet, wouldn't you?'

Lucy shrugged. 'That depends. If I were your pet, what would I have to do? I don't want to be your babysitter.'

Mila looked horrified. 'Of course you wouldn't be our babysitter!' she said. 'We don't need looking after.'

'So what would I have to do?'

'You should already know what pets do,' said Mila. 'You work in a pet shop, after all. All you have to do is be friendly and adorable.'

'Well, I'm good at looking adorable,' said Lucy. She tilted her head to one side and blinked her eyes a few times.

Mila clapped her hands. 'See? That's perfect!' she said. She grabbed Lucy by the hand. 'Come on. Let's go!'

'Hang on,' said Lucy, as though an idea had just struck her. 'How much will you pay me?'

'Pets don't get paid!' said Mila, sounding shocked. 'But . . . I'll buy you everything you need.'

Lucy's eyes gleamed. 'Everything?' she said slowly.

Mila nodded. 'Everything.'

The shopkeeper still didn't look pleased. 'Lucy is not a pet!' he said again. 'Plus I need her to help me in the shop.'

'Oh please, Dad,' said Lucy. 'It sounds like fun.'

Then Marcus had an idea. 'Maybe we could just borrow Lucy for the afternoon?' he suggested. 'It could be a trial run, just to see how it goes.'

Lucy nodded. 'That sounds like a great idea,' she said.

Mila thought about it. Then she nodded too. 'Sure,' she said.

Finally the shopkeeper agreed. 'OK,' he said. 'But this is the craziest idea I've ever heard.'

'Really?' said Mila, surprised. 'I think it makes perfect sense.'

CHAPTER FOUR

MILA PULLED Lucy along. 'Come on, Pickles,' she said. 'It's time to go.'

Lucy gave her a funny look. 'Why did you just call me Pickles?' she asked. 'My name's Lucy.'

'Not anymore,' said Mila. 'If you are our pet then you must be called Pickles. It's one of our Tinkler rules.'

Marcus had never heard this rule before.

'Well, don't say it too loudly,' said Lucy. She didn't look very happy about her new name.

'Can we go outside now?' asked Turtle.

'Hey, I've got a great idea!' said Mila. 'Let's take Pickles to the pet park.'

The pet park was a special place just for people with pets. The Tinklers had always wanted to go there.

Mila knelt down. 'Hop up on my shoulder, Pickles,' she said. 'I'll carry you there.'

'No way!' said Lucy.

'But you have to!' said Mila. 'You're my pet and you have to do what I say.'

Mila looked mad.

Lucy looked mad too.

'You know what, Mila?' said Marcus hastily. 'Well-trained pets walk along beside their owners.'

'Is that right?' said Mila. 'Well, of course Pickles is very well trained. She can walk along with us.'

Marcus soon found out that there was one good thing about having a teenager as a pet: They had no problems at all with Worried Adults. In fact, no-one even looked twice at them now that they had Lucy with them!

Maybe they think she is our babysitter, thought Marcus. He didn't say this to Mila, though. He knew she wouldn't like that one bit!

Turtle had decided she wanted to crawl to the park. But after a couple of blocks she suddenly stopped.

'I am too tired to a crawl any further,' she said.

'Why don't you walk then?' Marcus asked.

'Because I am a turtle,' said Turtle. 'Turtles crawl.'

'But you walked to the pet shop,' Marcus pointed out.

'That was different.'

Marcus didn't think it was different at all. But Turtle looked cranky. Have you ever tried arguing with a cross turtle? Here is some advice: **DON'T BOTHER.**

'At the pet shop, if we ever need our turtles to go anywhere, we pick them up and carry them,' said Lucy kindly. 'Would you like me to carry you for a while?'

Turtle nodded and reached up her arms. 'You are a great pet, Pickles,' she said.

Marcus was starting to think the same thing.

Lucy carried Turtle until they were almost at the park. Then she stopped and stared into a shop window.

'Why have you stopped, Pickles?' said Mila crossly. 'We're almost at the park.'

'I need a new pair of shoes,' said Lucy. She pointed to a pair in the shop window. 'I like those ones.'

Mila looked at the shoes and gasped. 'They're so expensive!' she said.

Lucy put Turtle down and folded her arms across her chest. 'You said you would buy me EVERYTHING I need,' she said. 'I need those shoes and I'm not going anywhere until I get them.'

Mila sighed. 'Well, OK,' she said. 'I have some pocket money with me. I guess I can buy you the shoes if you really need them.'

'I do,' said Lucy.

Lucy went into the shop with Mila. When they came out a few minutes later, Lucy was wearing new shoes. She looked happy. Mila did not look so happy.

'OK, Pickles,' Mila said. 'You have the shoes now. Can we finally go to the park?'

'Of course!' said Lucy. 'There's just one tiny problem.'

'What's that?' asked Mila.

'I don't have a hat,' said Lucy.

'A hat?' said Mila.

'It's very warm today,' said Lucy. 'I could get sunburnt.'

'It's terrible when pets get sunburnt,' said Turtle.

'Well, where am I going to get a hat from?' asked Mila.

Lucy pointed to a different shop. 'They have hats,' she said. 'They also have sunglasses.'

'Sunglasses?' repeated Mila. 'But you didn't say anything about sunglasses before.'

'Well, I'm saying it now,' said Lucy.

So Mila went into the shop and bought a hat and some sunglasses. She came back and gave them to Lucy.

'I hope that's everything you need,' she said.

Lucy put the hat and the sunglasses on. 'Oh yes, that's everything I need,' she said happily. 'For now, at any rate.'

★ ★ ★

CHAPTER FIVE

THE PARK was full of people and pets. There were dogs everywhere, running and jumping and barking.

There was a family in one of the paddleboats on the pond with their dog sitting up in the back. There was an old lady sitting on a bench in the sun with a cat asleep on her lap. Two little girls were hopping around after two pet rabbits.

Marcus even saw a boy with a rat on his shoulder.

Mila grabbed hold of Lucy's hand. 'Come on, Pickles,' she said. 'Let's walk around the pond together. I want everyone to see you.'

The Tinklers and Lucy walked all the way around the pond. Then they walked around it again. When they had gone around the pond three times, Lucy stopped.

'I'm tired of walking,' she said.

'Don't stop!' begged Mila. 'No-one has told me what a great pet you are.'

But Lucy wouldn't walk anymore. She sat down on a rock. 'I need a drink,' she said. 'And an ice-cream.'

'I need a drink and an ice-cream too,' said Turtle quickly.

'Me too!' said Marcus.

'But the kiosk queue is really long,' Mila complained.

'Well, you should join it now,' said Lucy, 'before it gets any longer.'

Mila sighed and joined the queue. She stood there for a very long time, but she finally came back with ice-creams and drinks for everyone. She looked very glum and Marcus could guess why. Mila had spent a lot of their pocket money. She didn't like doing that *at all*.

★ ★ ★

'What are *you* lot doing here?' said a nasty voice.

Marcus turned around to see the three Splatley children.

Sarah, Simon and Susie Splatley lived at thirty-three Rushby Road too. Their flat was on the thirty-first floor.

The Tinklers and the Splatleys were *not* friends. They were not even *close* to being friends.

I'll tell you why: The Splatleys were the meanest kids around. Their fingers were always ready to P*INCH* people and their mouths are always ready to say something N*ASTY*.

Sarah Splatley was holding a leash. And on the other end of it was a dog.

'Whose dog is that?' asked Marcus.

He thought it looked like a nice dog.

'He's ours,' said Sarah. 'We just got him.'

'You're lucky,' said Marcus. 'He looks like he'd be lots of fun to play with.'

Simon pulled a face. 'We don't *play* with him,' he said. 'We're too busy teaching him tricks. Fuzzby is extremely intelligent. He is probably the most intelligent pet in this whole park.'

'What tricks can he do?' asked Mila.

'He can catch a ball in his mouth,' said Simon proudly. 'Watch.'

Simon Splatley threw a tennis ball to the dog. The dog jumped up and caught the ball in his mouth.

'That's not such a big deal,' said Mila. 'Our pet can catch a ball in her hands.'

'You don't have a pet,' said Sarah.

'Yes, we do,' said Mila. 'We just got one today.'

'Where is it then?' asked Simon.

Mila pointed at Lucy.

Lucy waved at the Splatleys and smiled.

'Her name is Pickles,' said Mila.

'That's not a pet,' said Sarah. 'That's a teenager.'

'She's a *pet* teenager,' said Mila. 'And she's way smarter than your dog. She can CATCH a ball and then juggle it.'

'I can't actually juggle,' said Lucy.

'Oh,' said Mila, disappointed. 'But you can catch a ball, right?'

Lucy looked a little offended. 'Of course I can!'

Mila took the tennis ball from Fuzzby. Then she threw it to Lucy.

Lucy caught it and threw it back.

Mila threw the ball again. This time she threw it over Lucy's head and Lucy had to run to catch it.

This time when Lucy threw it back, she threw it very **HARD**.

Lucy looks a bit annoyed, thought Marcus.

But Mila didn't seem to notice. She threw the tennis ball again, as hard as she could.

'Run, Pickles, run!' she called.

But Lucy didn't run. Instead, she walked off very slowly after the ball. And when Lucy reached the ball, she didn't stop and pick it up. She walked straight past it!

'Pickles!' yelled Mila. 'The ball is RIGHT THERE!'

But Lucy didn't hear Mila. Or maybe she didn't *want* to hear her. She walked over to a group of teenage girls nearby. She sat down next to them. And soon, they were all laughing and chatting together.

'Ha ha,' said Simon Splatley. 'Your pet has run away.'

The Splatleys started to walk off, but Fuzzby ran back to the Tinklers. He licked Marcus's hand.

Marcus bent down and patted Fuzzby. 'You can come and visit us any time,' he said to the dog. 'We live on the thirty-third floor.'

'You Tinklers are crazy,' jeered Sarah. 'Everyone knows animals can't understand humans.'

'Maybe they can't,' shrugged Marcus. 'But then again, maybe they can.'

CHAPTER SIX

AFTER THE Splatleys had gone, Marcus looked at Mila. He was waiting for her to get really mad. Mila didn't like it when her plans went wrong. She especially didn't like looking silly in front of the Splatleys. She had a very thoughtful look on her face.

'What are you thinking about?' asked Marcus.

'I'm thinking that Pickles isn't the right pet for us, after all,' said Mila. 'She's a lot of work and costs too much money.' Mila coughed and rubbed her eyes. 'Plus, I think I'm a bit allergic to her.'

Marcus didn't think Mila was really allergic to Lucy. But he *did* think Lucy wasn't the right pet for them.

'So, what should we do with her?' he asked.

'Well, I guess we should take her back to the pet shop.'

Marcus didn't want to leave the park just yet. It was nice and sunny. There were kids playing football. Marcus felt like playing football too. Marcus also wanted to hire a paddleboat and go for a ride on the pond.

Marcus looked over at Lucy. She was still chatting with her friends. She didn't look like she wanted to leave, either.

'How about we just let her go free?' Marcus suggested.

'What do you mean?' asked Mila.

'We don't have to take her back to the pet shop,' explained Marcus. 'We can just set her free, right here in the park.'

'It is a bad idea to let pets loose in the wild,' said Turtle. 'There was a boy who let his goldfish loose in a lake once. The goldfish grew really huge and ate all the food in the lake. There was nothing left for any of the other fish.'

'You're right, Turtle,' said Mila. 'If we let Pickles loose in the park she would eat all the ice-cream. There would be none left for anyone else.'

'That won't happen,' said Marcus. 'She'd need lots of money to do that. She'll probably just go home when she's hungry.'

Mila thought about this for a while. Then she nodded and said, 'You're right, Marcus. I'll go and tell her she's free.'

Mila ran over to where Lucy was sitting. Marcus saw her say something to Lucy. Lucy listened and nodded. Then she and Mila shook hands.

After a few moments, Mila came back looking happy.

'It feels so good, setting things free,' she said. 'I want to buy another pet just so I can let it go too. Maybe a baby tiger.'

'Hmm. How much money do you have?' asked Marcus.

Mila pulled out her purse. 'I have five dollars.'

'That's not enough to buy a baby tiger,' said Marcus. 'But it *is* enough to hire a paddleboat.'

Marcus was fairly sure Mila would say no to that. But, to his surprise, she nodded.

'OK,' she said. 'Why not? I will save lots of money now I don't have to buy things for Pickles anymore.'

'That's true,' said Marcus.

The Tinklers spent the rest of the day in the park.

They rode around in the paddleboat.

They climbed trees.

They played football.

They stayed there until the sun began to set.

'Where is Turtle?' Mila asked.

Marcus looked around. Near a bench he saw Turtle's shell. Her legs were sticking up over the edge.

Marcus walked over and looked in. Turtle was fast asleep.

'We'd better take her home,' he said to Mila. 'You grab one end of the box and I'll grab the other.'

It was hard work, carrying Turtle home in her shell. But Marcus was glad that at least Mila hadn't tried to make him carry her on his own.

'Having Turtle is a bit like having a pet, don't you think?' said Mila.

'A little bit,' said Marcus. 'But don't ever tell Turtle that!'

CHAPTER SEVEN

TURTLE WOKE UP just as Marcus and Mila arrived back at thirty-three Rushby Road. She rubbed her eyes and sat up in her shell. 'I'm HUNGRY,' she said.

Marcus and Mila were hungry too. Luckily, there was a bakery on the ground floor of their building.

The bakers who worked there were called Barry and Betty. They loved giving tasty treats to the Tinklers.

'Did someone say they were hungry?' said Betty, popping out of the shop with a bag of goodies.

The Tinklers thanked Betty and took the bag upstairs. They ate the bakery treats for dinner. For dessert they had chocolate ice-cream.

The Tinklers always had chocolate ice-cream for dessert, except when they had chocolate ice-cream for their main course. On those days they had strawberry ice-cream for dessert instead.

'I've been thinking about what pet we should try next,' said Mila, as they cleared everything away. 'We want a pet that doesn't need any looking after at all.'

'All pets need a little looking after,' said Marcus.

'Are you sure?' said Mila. 'There must be at least one that doesn't need to be looked after.'

'You're right, there is!' said Marcus. He ran to the hallway and picked up a rock from the Tinklers' rock collection.

He quickly drew a face on it, then hurried back and gave it to Mila. 'Here you go,' he said.

'What's this?' asked Mila.

'It's a pet rock,' said Marcus. 'It's the perfect pet for you because it looks after itself. And you won't ever need to buy it anything.'

Mila put the rock down. 'Very funny, Marcus,' she said. 'But a rock is not the sort of pet I want at all.'

Later that evening, the Tinklers were in the lounge room together. Turtle was making a new shell. Marcus was reading a book about inventions. Mila was writing a list of animals that made good pets.

'What about a bat?' she said. 'They are pretty cute.'

But before Marcus could answer her, there came a noise. The Tinklers looked at each other.

'What was that?' said Mila.

'I think it was someone at the door,' said Marcus.

The Tinklers all went to the front door and opened it. Standing on the mat was the Splatley's dog. He looked up at the Tinklers and wagged his tail.

'Hi Fuzzby!' Marcus said. 'What are you doing here?'

The dog lifted up a paw.

'Look!' said Mila. 'He's got something balanced on his paw.'

It was a round bit of plastic, like a coin, but blue. Marcus picked it up.

'That's a Ludo token,' said Mila.

Marcus had a feeling he knew what was going on. 'Are the Splatleys trying to teach you Ludo?' he asked.

Fuzzby flopped down on the mat and put his paws over his eyes. He made a sound that was a lot like a groan.

Mila bent down and gave Fuzzby a pat. 'I know exactly how you feel. Ludo is the most boring game in the world, isn't it?'

Marcus bent down beside the dog too. 'Don't worry, Fuzzby,' he said. 'They always stop playing at eight o'clock. You can stay here until it's safe for you to go back down.'

Fuzzby stood up immediately and trotted happily into the Tinklers' flat.

He sniffed around for a moment, then lay down on the floor.

Mila scratched his belly. Then Fuzzby jumped up and licked Mila's face.

'Sit,' said Marcus.

Fuzzby sat and wagged his tail.

'Good dog,' said Marcus, giving him a scratch between the ears.

Turtle found a tennis ball, and Fuzzby had great fun chasing it all around the Tinklers' flat.

A few minutes later there was a knock at the door. It wasn't a polite knock. It was more of a rude **BANGING**. There were only three people in the world who banged on a door like that: THE SPLATLEY THREE.

'What have you done with our dog?' said Sarah Splatley as soon as Marcus opened the door.

'We haven't done anything with your dog,' said Mila. This was true. Fuzzby was asleep.

'You told him to come and visit you,' said Simon.

'But Simon,' said Mila, 'everyone knows that animals can't understand humans.'

Simon pulled a face but didn't say anything.

'Let us in!' demanded Sarah. 'We want to check if he's in there.'

And then Mila SNEEZED.

She always did this when she had an idea. Sometimes Mila's ideas were good, but sometimes they weren't. Marcus hoped that this was a *very* good one.

'Of course! Come in!' said Mila.

Oh no! thought Marcus. This was *not* one of Mila's good ideas.

'But we should warn you that we have a new pet,' Mila went on. 'In fact, we have lots of new pets.'

The Splatleys looked at the Tinklers suspiciously. 'What kind of pets?' asked Sarah.

'Spiders!' said Mila with a big grin. 'Oh, they are *SO* cute. They're huge and hairy, and they love jumping onto your head. Come in and meet them. They don't bite. Well, only a little bit.'

Sarah Spatley went very pale. Simon Splatley took a step back from the door. Little Susie Splatley started to blubber.

'We've changed our minds. We don't want to come in after all,' said Sarah quickly. 'We have to keep looking for our dog.'

'Good luck!' said Mila.

Marcus had to try very hard not to laugh as the Splatleys jumped into the lift and the doors closed.

Fuzzby stayed at the Tinklers' place until the clock chimed eight. Then he jumped down off the couch and licked each of the Tinklers' hands.

'I think he's saying thanks,' said Marcus.

'Of course he's saying that,' said Mila. She gave the dog a pat. 'You are welcome here any time,' she told Fuzzby.

The dog wagged his tail.

The Tinklers watched him trot off down the stairs.

'I think I have found my perfect pet,' said Mila.

'You mean Fuzzby?' said Marcus. 'But he belongs to the Splatleys.'

'That's why he's so perfect,' said Mila. 'The Splatleys have to do all the hard work of looking after him. We get to play with him in the evenings! That is JUST the kind of pet we need.'

★ ★ ★

INTRODUCING
the
TINKLERS
THREE

MARCUS

Age: Eight.

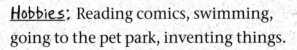

How to spot him: He's the kid who is always collecting things to use in his inventions.

Favourite place to escape: His workshop in the basement.

Hobbies: Reading comics, swimming, going to the pet park, inventing things.

Biggest dream: He'd like to invent the world's best mailbox.

Dislikes: Adults who think the Tinklers need a grown-up to look after them.

Favourite food: Cheese and pineapple pancakes (he invented these himself!).

Biggest secret: He isn't sure he wants to join the circus like his parents. He thinks he might like to be an inventor instead.

MILA

Age: Ten.

How to spot her: She's the girl with a bird's nest on her head.

Likes: Making up new rules.

Dislikes: Playing Ludo with the Splatley family.

Biggest dream: To make a bed she could wear so she would never have to get up.

Thing that annoys her most: Ice-cream should come in bigger tubs (bathtub size would be perfect!).

Current project: Doing special arm exercises so she can learn to fly.

When she grows up: Mila can't wait to join the circus like her parents.

Favourite thing to cook: Upside-down cake. She makes it while hanging upside down.

TURTLE

Age: Three.

How to spot her: She's the kid with a box tied to her back.

Why is she called Turtle? Because she thinks she is one.

Favourite book: *Big Book of Turtle Facts* (written by Mila Tinkler).

Favourite food: Something that starts with 'L' and ends with 'ettuce'.

Favourite things to play with: Boxes and sticks.

She is smart because: She already knows how to read and uses lots of big words.

She is not so smart because: She thinks turtles can growl and fetch sticks.

When she grows up: She wants to be a shark.

THE BAKERS

What they do: They run the bakery on the ground floor of thirty-three Rushby Road.

How to spot them: They are usually covered in flour.

Hobbies: Baking. Barry also likes playing cricket (he is a bowler).

BETTY

BARRY

Where do they live? Good question. Barry and Betty spend so much time at the bakery that they are not really sure where their house is!

Their motto: You can never have too much cake, too much bread or too many biscuits.

THE SPLATLEYS

SARAH

<u>Ages</u>: Ten (Sarah), eight (Simon), and three (Susie).

<u>How to spot them</u>: They are the ones doing something horrible.

<u>Hobbies</u>: Being sneaky and mean. Getting other people into trouble. Laughing when other people hurt themselves. Playing Ludo.

<u>Favourite food</u>: Anything they've snatched out of someone else's hand.

SIMON

SUSIE

The TINKLERS THREE

THREE MORE
ADVENTURES!

The TINKLERS THREE

a VERY *good* IDEA

M.C. BADGER

The TINKLERS THREE

an excellent INVENTION

M.C. BADGER

The TINKLERS THREE

the coolest TOOL

M.C. BADGER